Written by Deborah Guarino

Illustrated by Seth Hippen

Schiffer Kids™

4880 Lower Valley Road, Atglen, PA 19310

For my son,
Daniel Skyler,
whom I couldn't love more . . .
Sharon, Glen, Anthony, Adriane--
my beloved siblings four.
And for **Isaac** (my "Murray"),
"Size Nine," and **Mel Brooks,**
who together, forever,
inspired this book!
—DG

For **Karalenn, Kenzie, Kendyl,** and **Pip.**
Without whom, I'm afraid, my moorings would slip.
—SH

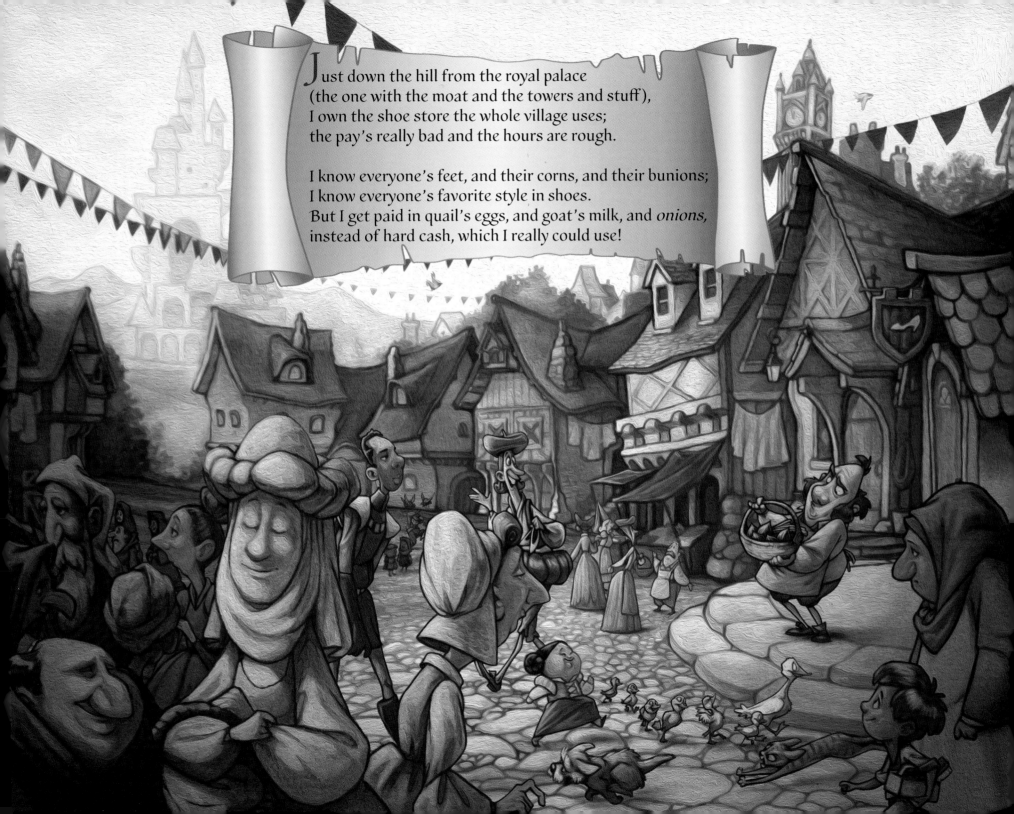

J ust down the hill from the royal palace
(the one with the moat and the towers and stuff),
I own the shoe store the whole village uses;
the pay's really bad and the hours are rough.

I know everyone's feet, and their corns, and their bunions;
I know everyone's favorite style in shoes.
But I get paid in quail's eggs, and goat's milk, and *onions,*
instead of hard cash, which I really could use!

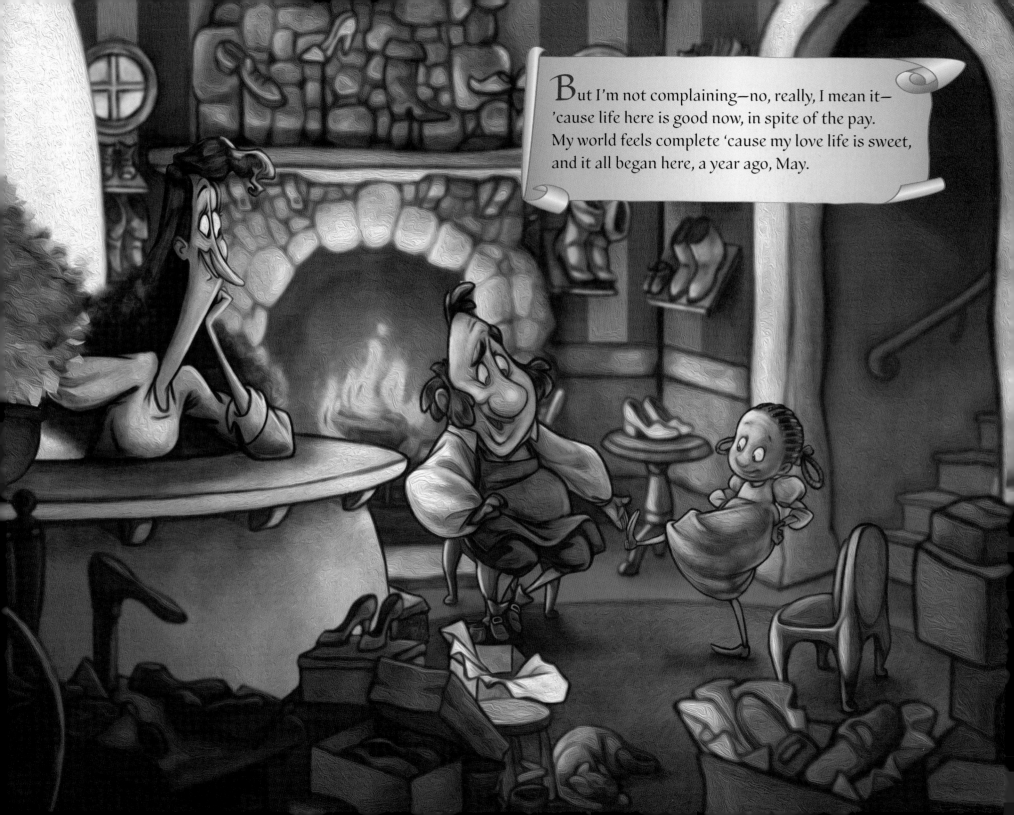

But I'm not complaining—no, really, I mean it—
'cause life here is good now, in spite of the pay.
My world feels complete 'cause my love life is sweet,
and it all began here, a year ago, May.

Late last spring, after shutting the store,
I heard a commotion downstairs, by the door.
When I opened up, to my surprise . . .

. . . a large fairy hovered before my eyes!
"Thank goodness!" she cried, waving her wand.
"I'm all out of magic, I can't go on!"
"Sorry," I said, a little confused.
"I don't sell magic . . . I just sell shoes."

"Perfect!" she said. "I've got this godchild—
she's pretty, she's sweet, she's meek, and she's mild,
but she lives with this horrible step-family, see,
and I've got to save her, it's all up to me!

So I used all my magic; I made her a gown . . .
I made her a carriage, some horses, a crown!
She looks such a picture, this girl cannot lose.
But wouldn't you know it? I forgot to make *shoes!*
The poor kid is barefoot, and—worst of all—
now she's late for the royal ball!"

I could see that this fairy was fairly chagrined,
so I said, "Fancy shoes? Don't worry, you're in!
I've got satin ones, silk ones, I've got ones with lace . . ."

But she just shook her head, a frown on her face.
"No, no, those won't do—I need a *rare* pair . . .
slippers as light and transparent as *air.*"

"Ah!" I said, smiling. "Is that all you ask?
I've got some in back! Size five . . . made of glass."
That fairy was enchanted! She said she'd pay well
as soon as she recharged her magic and spells.

I watched as she went to the carriage outside
and handed the shoes to the beauty with pride.
Then the horses sped off with the girl to the ball,
the fairy flew off, and I thought that was all.

But the very next day, when I opened the store,
Mona, my clerk, rushed through the door.
(Have I mentioned Mona yet? I haven't? Oh, gee . . .
Well, the truth is, she meant the world to me!)
I'd been too shy to tell her, but, right from the start,
she'd completely, totally, stolen my heart.

Unfortunately, Mona was always convinced
that she was destined to marry a *prince!*
Now she announced it was all over town . . .
"The prince is going to offer his crown!
He fell in love at the royal ball
with a beauty, they say—but that's not all!

Just as he starts to propose marriage,
she takes off in a magical, fancy carriage!
All he has now is her glass shoe, poor guy.
Oh, I wish he'd ask me," she said with a sigh.

"Well, what do you know about that?" I said.
"My glass slipper's famous!"
(It went straight to my head.)

"*You* made that shoe?!" Mona shrieked in my ear.
"You created that glass slipper *here?!*
Oh, Murray, my hero! This means there's a way
that *I* can become a princess today!"

"Huh?" was the only reply I could make.
Had Mona gone crazy? Was there some mistake?
"The foot the prince seeks is small and refined,
and though yours is lovely, dear . . . it's a size *nine!*"

"That doesn't matter, Murray, 'cause you
can easily make another glass shoe.
But this one you'll make for a foot just like mine—
a delicate slipper, all glass, and size nine!"

Well!
This was a pickle . . . what to do, what to do?
Mona wanted me to commit counterfeit with a shoe!
She still had that dream and now was convinced
that this was her one chance to marry a prince!

If I said no, all her hopes would be spoiled . . .
So, 'cause I loved her and have always been loyal,
"Okay," I said sadly, "I'll do it for you.
You watch the store while I make your glass shoe."
Then, heaving a sigh, I began the sad task,
completing, by noon, the new slipper of glass.

Mona grabbed it with glee—then, can you guess?
The prince and his entourage, tired from their quest,
arrived at my store, looking far from their best.

"We've been searching," a page yawned, "far and wide,
for the hand—and foot—of the prince's true bride.
So put your best foot forward, Miss.
Your future may depend on this."

"Oh, yes, yes, *yes!*" Mona said, almost swooning.
"I can't *wait* to begin the honeymooning!"

This woke everyone up, and their eyes grew round
as they looked Mona up and they looked Mona down.
Then they looked at each other and presented the shoe,
and Mona did what I dreaded but knew that she'd do.

She took their glass slipper, then casually coughed.
"Oh, look, a *smudge*," she said, rubbing it off.
And as she polished the shoe with a soft, shammy rag,
she replaced it with *hers*, putting *theirs* in a bag.

Then, with a smile, her large foot extended,
she slipped on the *new* shoe . . .
"Prince! *I'm* your intended!"

Mona leapt up with joy! The prince leapt back in fright.
"Are you sure about that? Something doesn't seem right.
Last night you looked different . . . your hair was all curled.
You looked smaller—and *younger*—are you the same girl?"

"Well, of course!" Mona lied. "The lighting was bad.
But it's still me, darling . . . now tell me you're glad!"

"Oh, uh, certainly, certainly," the prince said with a bow
(but he looked much paler and shaky, now).
His entourage groaned and his entourage gasped.
"Has the prince gone mad?" I heard someone ask.
"A deal's a deal," someone else persisted.
"If the shoe fits, that's it!" another insisted.
I guess the prince heard them, because, with a sigh,
he kissed Mona's hand, and then—what a guy!—
made it official: "Here is my bride."

Well, with that announcement, what an intrusion!
Reporters burst in! There was chaos, confusion!
There was shoving and pushing . . . I got a *contusion!*

When the dust had settled, my Mona was gone.
"Oh, no," I thought. "What have I *done?*

The prince doesn't love Mona . . .
what to do, what to do?
All of this trouble because of a *shoe?!*"

Then, as if things couldn't *get* more depressing,
the fairy flew in, outraged and protesting.
"What goes on here?" she cried.
"What's the holdup, what gives?
Why isn't the prince where my goddaughter lives?"

"Uh . . ." was all I could think of to say.
"Something came up and he went on his way.
He found his bride in my store today."

"His bride? His *bride?!*" the fairy sputtered.
Her face turned red and both wings fluttered.
"The prince's bride lives way across town!
What fraud *dares* to steal her crown?!"

I have to admit I was really afraid
to confess about the glass shoe that I made.
But after explaining I'd done it for love,
for someone I happened to think the world of,
the fairy, a romantic, actually *listened*,
'til both wings drooped and her violet eyes glistened.

"Oh, you wonderful man," she sobbed at last.
"You didn't just make a slipper of glass . . .
You sacrificed your own true love
so that *she* would be happy . . . oh, you great big lug!"

"Then you're not angry?" I said. "You understand?
You'll let the prince have Mona's hand?"

"Of *course* not! Are you *crazy?!*" the irate fairy asked.
"There's still just one foot for that shoe made of glass!"

Then she preened both her wings.
"Come on, no more fretting!
I've got a plan to disband this whole wedding!"

With a stroke of her wand—now loaded with power—
she transported us both to the palace tower!

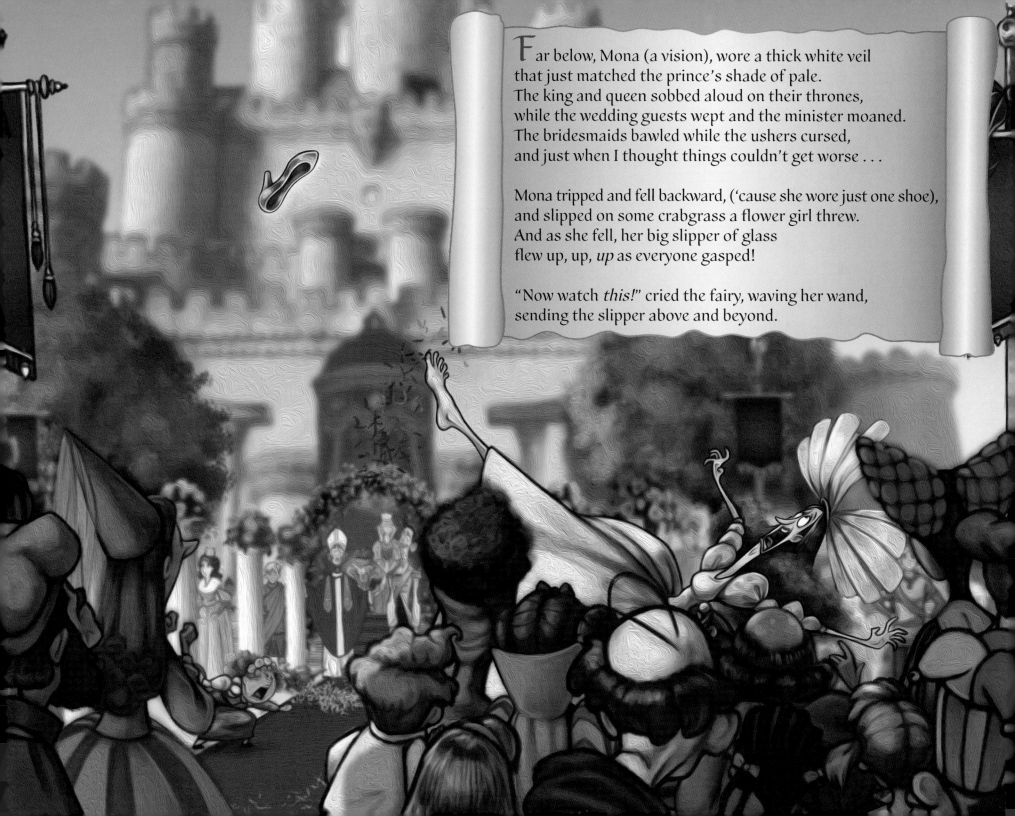

Far below, Mona (a vision), wore a thick white veil
that just matched the prince's shade of pale.
The king and queen sobbed aloud on their thrones,
while the wedding guests wept and the minister moaned.
The bridesmaids bawled while the ushers cursed,
and just when I thought things couldn't get worse . . .

Mona tripped and fell backward, ('cause she wore just one shoe),
and slipped on some crabgrass a flower girl threw.
And as she fell, her big slipper of glass
flew up, up, *up* as everyone gasped!

"Now watch *this!*" cried the fairy, waving her wand,
sending the slipper above and beyond.

Defying gravity, it soared through the sky,
where I reached out and caught it on the fly!
"Well done!" said the fairy, floating us down,
ignoring the throng now gathered around.
Then she switched the size nine for the real shoe, size five
in front of poor Mona's incredulous eyes.

"Here you are, dear," the fairy said sweetly.
"This tiny glass slipper should fit you quite neatly."

"Oh, no . . . now it's dirty," Mona said, thinking fast.
"I can't *possibly* marry wearing smudged glass."

"Is there a problem?" the prince asked, "I really don't mind.
I can wait a few *years* . . . please, take your time."

"Don't be silly, my darling," Mona soothed.
"I'll get married barefoot! Who needs an old shoe?"

"YOU do!" bellowed the King, "and let it be said
if that shoe *doesn't* fit, it's OFF with your head!"

Mona's bare toes quivered, they quavered, they shook.
If I didn't save her, her goose would be cooked!

"It's *my* fault!" I shouted. "Blame only *me*!
This is a crime of the heart, don't you see?
She wanted you, prince, so I made a false shoe.
I thought when you met her, you'd want Mona, too.
But you *don't*, do you?" I whispered, leaning close to his ear.
(I didn't want my poor Mona to hear.)

"Well, of course he doesn't, that's part of my spell!"
interrupted the fairy, starting to yell.
"You can't interfere with the workings of fate,
no matter how many fake slippers you make.
The prince must go now to my goddaughter's house.
She'll need a good bath, but she's his true spouse!"

"What a relief!" the grateful prince sighed.
"Forgive them, Dad . . . I'll go fetch the real bride!"

Then, with a sweep of his cloak, he departed,
leaving my Mona, I thought, broken-hearted.

But instead of sobbing, my Mona was *smiling*,
and looking at *me* in a way quite beguiling.
Was something wrong? Was my Mona demented?
Why was a girl who got dumped so contented?

"I'll tell you, Murray," that large fairy said,
reading the unspoken thoughts in my head.
"There was still a matter of that unpaid sale
for a glass shoe used in a fairy tale.
I always pay my debts, and so,
I cast a spell upon your beau."

"But I don't want her through magic, I want her for *real*,"
I said from my heart. "Or else it's no deal!"

"But I *do* love you for real, Murray dear," Mona said.
"The fairy's spell just cleared my head
of daydreams and bad schemes and a fairy-tale prince."

"Are you kidding?" I asked her (I still wasn't convinced).
"You're over it *all?* The prince, the glass shoe?"
"Over and done with," Mona smiled. "I love *you*."

So that is our tale, Mona's and mine.
We got married, we're happy, we're doing just fine.
And our proudest possession is a pair of sublime,
but mismatched glass slippers . . .
size five and size nine!

Other Schiffer Books on Related Subjects:
Shoes, Little Shoes, Big Shoes, Ester Llorens & Jordi Palet, ISBN 978-0-7643-5687-2
They Turned Me Down!, Ester Llorens & Jordi Palet, ISBN 978-0-7643-5689-6

Library of Congress Control Number: 2019935799

Set of old blank scrolls paper on white background vector image © dualororua. Courtesy of Vectorstock.
Cover design by Jack Chappell
Type set in Raustila/Times

ISBN: 978-0-7643-5843-2 (hard cover)
ISBN: 978-0-7643-5882-1 (soft cover)
Printed in China

Published by Schiffer Kids
An imprint of Schiffer Publishing, Ltd.
4880 Lower Valley Road
Atglen, PA 19310
Phone: (610) 593-1777; Fax: (610) 593-2002
E-mail: Info@schifferbooks.com
Web: www.schifferbooks.com

For our complete selection of fine books on this and related subjects, please visit our website at www.schifferbooks.com. You may also write for a free catalog.

Schiffer Publishing's titles are available at special discounts for bulk purchases for sales promotions or premiums. Special editions, including personalized covers, corporate imprints, and excerpts, can be created in large quantities for special needs. For more information, contact the publisher.

We are always looking for people to write books on new and related subjects. If you have an idea for a book, please contact us at proposals@schifferbooks.com.